WS

D0514334

C04 - S297

For Joe Douglas
I.W.

For Mum
love David

British Library Cataloguing in Publication Data
A catalogue record of this book is available from the British Library.

ISBN 0 340 79198 5 (HB)
ISBN 0 340 79199 3 (PB)

Text copyright © Ian Whybrow 2001
Illustrations copyright © David Melling 2001

The right of Ian Whybrow to be identified as the author
and David Melling as the illustrator of this Work
has been asserted by them in accordance with
the Copyright, Designs and Patents Act 1988

First published in 2001
by Hodder Children's Books,
a division of Hodder Headline Limited,
338 Euston Road, London NW1 3BH

10 9 8 7 6 5

Printed in Hong Kong

All rights reserved

All Change!

Written by Ian Whybrow

Illustrated by David Melling

Hodder
Children's
Books

A division of Hodder Headline Limited

WORCESTERSHIRE COUNTY COUNCIL
CULTURAL SERVICES

It was the tiger's birthday
And he was quite upset.
Miss Lollipop said, 'There, there!
You're making me all wet.'
'I didn't get a present,'
The tearful tiger sighed.

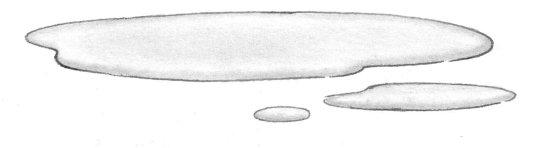

Miss Lollipop said, 'Cheer up!
We'll go for a birthday ride!'

That was just what the tiger wanted
So they drove down a country lane.
Miss Lollipop shouted, 'All change!'
And they jumped aboard . . .

. . . a train.

They stopped at a seaside station
And picked up a billy goat.
The goat bleated, 'All change!'
So they jumped into ...

. . . a boat.

They rowed to where the seals live
And then put up the sail.
A seal barked, 'All change!'
And they jumped into . . .

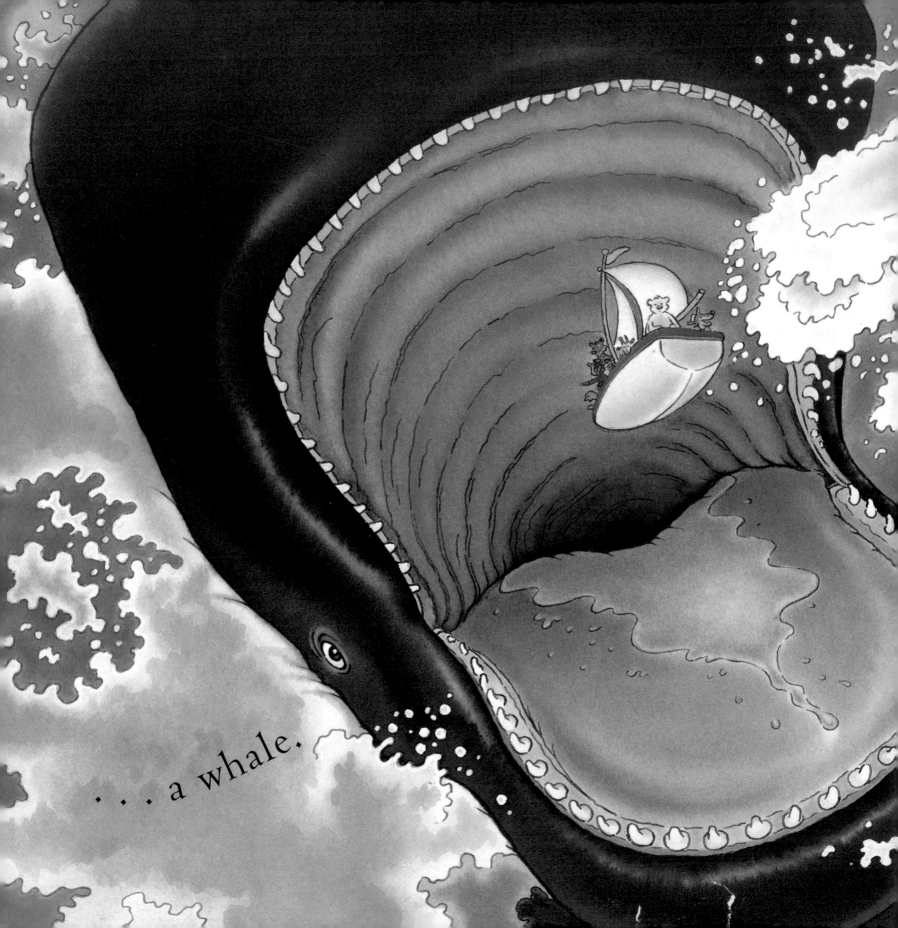

. . . a whale.

They rumbled in his tummy
And gave the whale a pain.
So he blew them all out through his spout
And they jumped into . . .

. . . a plane.

The plane flew high up in the sky.
Then they had a bit of luck.

The pilot shouted, 'All change!'
And they landed in . . .

. . . a dumper truck.

The dumper truck went bumpety bump
Which is just what animals like.
The puffin shouted,
'All change!'
And they jumped onto . . .

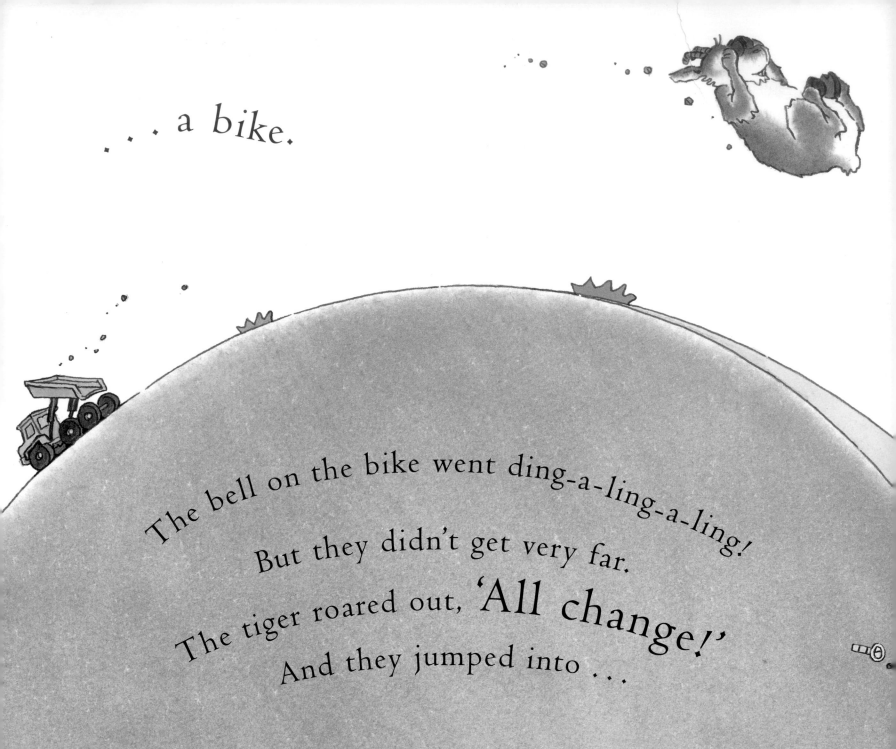

... a bike.

The bell on the bike went ding-a-ling-a-ling!
But they didn't get very far.
The tiger roared out, 'All change!'
And they jumped into ...

. . . a racing car.

The racing car went brrrm, brrrm, brrrm,
As round the track it sped.
The animals yawned and said, 'All change!'
Then they all jumped into . . .

Wait a minute, wait a minute!
What did they change into?

Yes! They changed into their pyjamas!
But . . . wait a minute, wait a minute!
Then what did they do?

Yes! They helped the tiger open all his presents . . . and then they all had a piece of the tiger's birthday cake . . .

And at last the animals cleaned their teeth
and this is what they said:

'Night, night, Miss Lollipop!'
And they jumped into their · · ·

. . . bed!